One day Waggle-Tail, the s.
terrible fright. He ran away from the others, because
he wanted to see if there was a puddle he could swim
on all by himself. The pond seemed so crowded, when
all the white ducks and the yellow ducklings were
on it.

Well, Waggle-Tail waddled off
to where he saw the rain-puddle
shining. It was a very nice
puddle indeed. Waggle-
Tail sat on it and did a little
swim all round it, quacking
in his small duckling-voice.

The farm-cat heard him and left his seat on the wall at once. Young fat ducklings made wonderful dinners for cats — but usually the ducklings kept with the big ducks and the farm-cat was afraid then.

'A duckling on a puddle by itself!' said the big black cat to himself in joy. He crept round by the wall. He crept round the pig-sty. He crouched low and waggled his body ready to jump — and just then the duckling saw him. With a terrified quack, he scrambled off the puddle and ran to find his mother.

But he went the wrong way, poor little thing. He went under the field-gate instead of under the gate that led to the pond. The cat crept after him, his tail swinging from side to side.

'Quack! Quack! Quack!' cried the yellow duckling. 'Quack! Quack! Quack!'

But his mother didn't hear him. Nobody heard him — but wait! Yes — somebody *has* heard him! It is Bobbin the little rabbit!

Bobbin heard the duckling's quacking and popped his long ears out of his burrow. He saw Waggle-Tail waddling along — and he saw the farm-cat after him.

'Waggle-Tail, Waggle-Tail, get into my burrow, quickly!' cried Bobbin. Waggle-Tail heard him and waddled to the burrow. The cat would have caught him before he got there, if Bobbin hadn't leapt out and jumped right over the cat, giving him such a fright that he stopped for just a moment.

And in that moment, the little duckling was able to

run into the rabbit's hole! Down the dark burrow he waddled, quacking loudly, giving all the rabbits there *such* a surprise!

Bobbin leapt into the hole too and the friends sat side by side, wondering if the cat was still outside.

'I daren't go out, I daren't go out,' quacked poor Waggle-Tail.

'I will go and fetch your big white mother-duck,' said Bobbin. 'I can go out to the pond by the hole that leads there. Stay here for a little while.'

Bobbin ran down another hole and up a burrow that led to the bank of the pond. He popped out his furry head and called to Waggle-Tail's mother.

'The cat nearly caught Waggle-Tail. He is down my burrow. Please come and fetch him.' So the big white duck waddled from the pond to fetch her duckling from Bobbin's burrow. She was very grateful to Bobbin for saving her little Waggle-Tail.

'Maybe some day I shall be able to do you a good turn,' she said. And off she went, quacking loudly. Now not long after that, Bobbin wanted to go and see Waggle-Tail but, when he put his nose out of the burrow, he found that it was raining very hard.

'You must not go out in that rain,' said his mother. 'Wait till it stops.'

But it didn't stop. The rain went on and on. Bobbin was very cross. 'I will borrow an umbrella,' he thought. So he went to his Great-aunt Jemima and was just going to ask her for an umbrella which was standing in the corner, when he saw that she was fast asleep.

Bobbin knew that no one should borrow things without asking, but he couldn't wait until Aunt Jemima woke up. So he tiptoed to the corner and took the big old umbrella.

He scuttled up the burrow with it, dragging it behind him. He pulled it out of the hole and put it up. My goodness, it *was* a big one!

Bobbin held on to the big crook-handle and set off down the hillside. It was a very windy day and the big purple clouds slid swiftly across the sky. A great gust of wind came, took hold of the umbrella — and blew it up into the sky!

And Bobbin went with it! He was such a little rabbit that the wind swept him right off his feet with the umbrella — and there he was, flying along in the sky, holding on to the umbrella!

He was dreadfully frightened. He clung to the handle with his two paws, hoping that he wouldn't fall but feeling quite sure he would, very soon. Poor Bobbin!

The wind swept him right over the pond. The ducklings looked up in surprise when they saw the enormous umbrella — but how they stared when they saw poor Bobbin hanging on to it too!

'It's a rabbit, it's a rabbit!' they cried. And Waggle-Tail knew which rabbit it was. 'It's Bobbin, my dear friend Bobbin!' quacked Waggle-Tail. 'Mother, Mother, look at Bobbin! He will fall. What can we do to save Bobbin? He saved me — we must save him!'

'But how can we?' said the mother-duck.

'Mother, can't you fly after him?' cried Waggle-Tail.
'I know you don't often fly, because you prefer to swim
— but couldn't you just *try* to fly after poor Bobbin?'

'I will try,' said the big mother-duck. So she spread
her big white wings and rose into the air. She flapped
her wings and flew after the big umbrella. Bobbin was
still holding on but his paws were getting so tired, that
he knew he would have to fall very soon.

The mother-duck flew faster and faster on her great wings. She caught up with the umbrella. She flew under the surprised rabbit and quacked to him.
'Sit on my back! Sit on my back!'